Cookies and Milk

With

a Book of Poetry

Preface

This collection of poetry is inspired by the words and surroundings I see every day. I hope you enjoy it as much as I did writing the poems.

Dedication
To my grandchildren
Shane, Isabelle, Jonathan,
Carter, Alexandra, Melanie,
Mollie and Madison

.

In Memory of
Herman S. Rubin
Who wrote poetry all his life.

Table Contents of

end of an era/error

tired of waiting
for him to leave,
she drives
to the train station
for the Amtrak
City of New Orleans
to take her mistake back home

standing still

she felt vibrations
on her feet
as the locomotive
rounds the bend,
coming into the station
whizzing past,
blowing her hat off
flying in the air,
landing on the platform

years ago, they dated;
recently, he called
trying to rekindle a romance

she forgot
how he denigrated her
with attitude and language

as the train pulls away
he waves.
she returns the wave,
just not using
all her fingers

a love story

the bullet pierces her heart-
but it is too late;
she died years ago
when she fell in love
with him

the flowers
followed chocolates,
plus gifts of gold
too expensive
for her to buy

he became irresistible,
serenaded
with love songs
in her native language,
she could not refuse him

it was a slow love
on her part
he was not tall
or good looking,
yet very charming

it took time,
she was seduced
by money and cars,
with long vacations
she only dreamed about

finally, he bought
a house for her
overlooking
the city below

things went well
until the third child
came along;
he lost interest
in being with her

Tijuana beckoned
just over the border.
he said he had
business there;
in too many brothels

alone and rejected,
she stepped out
to find new friends
and lovers,
a secret life for her

over the years
she had two more
children, not his,
he did not know or care
but kept her, as habits do

he came home one day,
she was out and about
filling her days
with new found loves,
as he did in Mexico

a friend told him
where she played;
waiting at home
he stewed and drank
until she walked in

one shot was all it took-
her life was over,
his soon would be too;
distraught from booze
he swallowed a bullet

there is no moral
to this story,
love can be immoral
and vile,
ending in tragedy for all

retirement community

living in a senior development
is great; on a golf course
for open views, no lawn troubles
or pool cleanings anymore

meeting new people
from all walks of life,
careers and ethnicities
make it interesting

the community
is a quarter-century old,
the people are transient,

i meet them in passing

goodbye

i saw a whale
breach the rough seas
of the North Atlantic,
shooting plumes of mist
high in the air,
then dive deep
flipping a tail
goodbye

i saw you
breach his heart,
an argument
between lovers
spewing
harsh words
in the air-
then you left
flipping him
a figurative
goodbye

as the whale
disappeared
from sight forever,
so did you

voluptuous

no apologies,
her body is fantastic,
all of it;
all of it with
every extra
pound of it

the big girl
heard it all
on the school bus
till her senior year-
it lost its sting
no longer biting

self-aware,
now confident,
she burst into maturity
enjoying it all,
in demand by men

precious treasures

they play in schoolyards
impervious in their small world
to the politics of the day;
unaware of policies
which imperil their future

climate change,
opioid addiction,
medical coverage,
poisoned water

regulations are a burden
to people and business,
but they have an underlying
fact, we must do everything we can
to protect our nation's young treasures

transparent democracy

we walk barefoot
on the hot sand
to the right spot
close to the ocean,
throw a blanket
down, our clothes
landing on top

gunnison beach
welcomes nudists,
every size, shape,
sex, and inclinations

around us are
school principals,
a town mayor,
a reverend, plus
a few harlots
sunning and smiling

at the nude beach
everyone is equal,
none better or worse
when nothing
is hidden-
all exposed,
it is a true
transparent democracy

soul-bearing

looking back
at another time,
we could be lovers
maybe married

it did not happen;
i was too young
and immature
when we dated-
i ghosted you

truth is
i liked you
a lot,
still do;
i know
it's too late
to change things

but today
decades later,
i can say
there are regrets

forgive me

the all-gender bathroom at Rutgers University

i went in to pee
and came out a we,
yes, it is still me
can't you see!
i'm finally free
i said with glee
it's really me,
all of we-
no need to flee
i have the key
to being we,
just go in to pee!

morning walk

on a chilled
february morning
my thoughts
rummage
in my mind,
when i hear a
tap tap
tap tap tap;
i stop
to see
where the sound
is coming from

on a small barren
gray tree,
perched way up
on a rather thin
long branch,
a woodpecker
is hard at work;
reminds me
of the times
i knocked my head
against opportunities,
which sometimes
worked out great,
and sometimes didn't;
at least i tried

real love

does it matter
what her skin color is
when my fingers
glide over,
my lips
softly
meet hers
pressing them,
when our bodies
gently mesh
merging clouds
of love
into their heavenly bliss,
leaving earth
taking us
to a dimension
of love,
unknown
before?

is love a wish

caring for another,
wanting to be wanted,
cared for,
to fill
an unfilled,
unexplained,
desire
burning hot
between two people

just a wish
subconsciously
to find love
between their
raging
uncontrollable hormones

death tragedies

the first tragedy-
when a child dies
the future dies too.
a parent's love
never decreases
but hurts forever-
hope, aspirations
are never attained
when a child dies

the second tragedy-
when an adult dies
in midlife
families torn apart,
fulfillment
of potential is lost
when an adult dies

the third tragedy-
when a senior dies
life experiences,
their knowledge
is buried with them
never passed along
to future generations,
when a senior dies

death is a tragedy
at any age

addicted to Johnnie

she stumbles out of the liquor store
clutching Johnnie by the neck
placing a brown paper bag
on a seat before driving off

in a trailer, her boyfriend
of the week watches her kids,
she never thinks 'bout them;
only where she can stop
to lick her lips with Johnnie
till nothings left to drink

police knock on her car window
she blacked out; they open the door,
take her away, and remove her car
from the middle of an intersection

after court, she goes home to find
her kids gone, the home stripped bare,
only empties strewn about-
bottomed out, she goes to rehab

it takes time to get sober-
work a job, kids back home,
everything going well, she stops for coffee,
is hit by a drunk driver, then dies on the spot

a letter

she married many times in life
not because she wanted-
her first love left
after a terrible fight

offered a job far away
she didn't want to go,
too far from home and mother,
where she did not know anyone

as he left, she told him to write
with an apology and proposal,
if not, then she was through;
her pride overcame her heart

thirty years, three marriages later
a letter came-
a postmark so many years old
it finally found its way

a proposal and apology inside
with words of sorrow, and love;
the tears of years came back
along with sharp chest pains

doctors tried to save her
their skills are not enough-
in heaven souls unite up high
as bodies are buried deep

mechanical life

my windshield wipers
slide from left to right
back and forth
never missing a beat-
in rhythm to the storm
as my eyes fight
to see
through blurred glass
until the rain stopped
wipers off

she is dangerous
but her charisma
ensnared me,
bringing lust
into my life-
a force of nature
i did not understand
could not control

our arguments
were like wipers,
going back and forth-
i'd say something
she'd respond
the issue still
blurring our feelings
until she stopped-
walked out,
ending it forever

Boulder Colorado

the city is so high
clouds seem so low,
if i raise my arms, i can
catch the floating white puffs

the early morning sun shines bright,
by afternoon grey clouds pop up
bringing drizzle and winds, turning
a downpour into a torrent

lightning flashes, thunder booms,
so loud the deaf can hear, now
throwing hail down pinging my car
causing me to park in a nearby lot

the rain ceases, bringing out the sun
when a flash flood cascades
down from the mountains,
washing away anything in its path

the river in the streets
stops and dries, as the sun
bakes the asphalt, allowing
me to continue on my way

in Boulder Colorado
if you don't like the
weather, wait ten minutes,
it will soon change

lingering scent

she was here
but left hours ago
for an appointment;
yet my mind still feels
her presence, as if,
she is still in my bed-
we were together, lovers,
many times before

when i rub my hand on
her side of the bed
the sheets release
her pheromones,
my senses
absorbing them
breaking my heart,
desiring to be with her still

my love life
twists and turns,
continuity
is not guaranteed

to experience her love again
nothing would stop me,
even if i have to pay
for additional time
with her

zombie village

i see them every day
walking the streets,
driving cars,
eating in places,
nothing to do
but shop and talk
talk and shop,
dream of past deeds
waiting to die,
living in retirement
amongst the living

alone

winter weather
can be as freezing
as his heart,
with no warmth
in the forecast

walking out
leaving behind
two young kids,
a sickly wife,
he heads for the warmth
of a mistress;
only to eventually find
she is as cold
emotionally as he is,
if not colder

as a sickly old man,
alone,
with no family,
living in a hospice
looking out at people
walking along
hand in hand,
he shuffles
into the hall
to a nurse's
pill station,
swallows a handful
of unknown meds

in his room, back in bed,
he closes his eyes,
for one last time

valentine's day

husbands cry
a child killed,
moms cry
a child's killed,
wives cry
a husband's killed,
sons cry
a parent's killed
siblings cry
a sibling's killed

drunk drivers
killed them,
politicians
killed them,
curable disease
killed them,
lack of medical care
killed them

yes,
valentine hearts
are red;
they are
bleeding hearts

music of love

lying in bed
she mentions
how the music
she played last
night was great

remember he said
it is the conductor
who leads the
orchestra playing
great music

she replied
that may be true,
but without
talented musicians
the conductor is
left playing the
music with himself

he surrendered,
and gave
her his baton
to lead
the orchestra tonight

the star

this symbol inspires with
intense devotion of faith,
yet amongst so many, also
unbridled, unleashed hatred

it comes in many colors,
done in precious stones,
silver or gold and even
platinum hanging on chains, even
concrete or wood on buildings

it once was made
in yellow fabric sewn on clothes
to humiliate and denigrate
it's wearer until they were killed

in a world of 15 billion only
15 million can wear this symbol,
so few,
so very few,
so hated
yet admired and envied

a symbol of antiquities
still breathing,
still proud,
still here

discussion

he said
your light went somewhere
bringing total darkness
to my heart, tearing out my
soul, losing your love forever

although your body is here
i can feel the emptiness
in your life-force, the flatness
in your voice, and the
ambivalence in your attitude

we had something great-
i don't know what I did to
change your feelings 'bout me.
tell me what I did to you, please

she said
truth is i am not happy-
i met someone else and
am attracted to this person-
i didn't expect it.
we met and fell in love.
i'm sorry, there is
magic about her
you don't have

love cycle

he thought
she would stay,
not leave him

in his narcissistic
mind he is a catch,
irreplaceable

trouble is
she thought
he is replaceable

in her mind
she is a catch-
no need to put up
with his issues

unfortunately,
he caught the eye
of another girl
starting the cycle again

fortunately,
she caught
the eye
of another lover-
happily, the two
girls are in love

doing the right thing

a naturalization ceremony
formally
makes foreign soldiers
citizens of the country
they served,
with all its benefits
and obligations

on this army base
in North Carolina
Senator McCain attended,
giving more import
to the ceremony;
the President probably
played golf that day

their names are
called individually-
they all served
with honor and distinction

in front
of the reviewing stands
rows of boots
are lined up

in their memory,
for the honor

mom's childhood wish

people can surprise you

when you think
you know them
something pops up
you never
in your wildest dreams
expected

i thought i knew
my mom-
she grew up
in the roaring 1920s
into the 1930s
in urban Brooklyn;
as a daughter,
wife, then a mother

she traveled
all across the world
from Asia to Africa
to Israel;
but there was still
one thing
she always wanted to do

on her deathbed she spoke
of a childhood desire
never fulfilled

the flying barnstormers
of her youth influenced her;
she wanted to fly
a plane by herself

divorce

being alone
is better
then being with you

those years
were misery
for me

i know soon,
just around the corner,
a great love is waiting

to restart my emotions,
beginning to love again,
without you

memories of love

when our lips
tenderly met
your kisses burned,
they set me on fire
when we are together
igniting a fury of love
not many experience

a storm of desire
overcomes me
i never
felt before

the day we met
is cherished,
remembered,
never forgotten

i curse
the day
you died

a south jersey blond

floating in
on whispering footsteps
she appeared
next to me as
if by magic,
a chilled basement
meeting room
warmed with her smile,
light reflecting
off the jewel
on her nose;
a face framed
with wisps of blond hair
resting on two shoulders;
blue eyes peering
behind dark-rimmed glasses,
with torn jeans
exposing patterned blue leggings-
her clothes cover talent
in a gifted, mature mind
back to the group
after years away-
she paints with words
how colors are seen;
truths not spoken, but
truth none the less,
on canvas and paper
her images fly into sight

short skirts

it did not matter
how short
her skirt is,
she had confidence
in herself,
showing it to all
most nights,
as she danced
with the pole
while men threw money
on stage,
hoping
she would show them
affection,
maybe even a lap dance
or two-
depending
on their generosity
they might even
walk together
to the v.i.p. room
for a private,
possibly illegal,
lap dance of sorts-
going home
in the early morning hours
with a pocketbook
overflowing
with unreported cash,
enabling her
to buy more
short skirts

a poetry group

they were all poets,
sitting around, reading
their poems, pens out
to critique the others

waiting their turn to read,
then listen, what others in
the room said of their work;
writing notes of improvement

opinions varied, some liked
it, others not so much,
changes suggested; its
the author's choice to accept

each week they meet,
corduroy and wine, penny
loafers too, very cerebral-
after all, it is in Princeton

i saw

i saw the results of war
in st. albans naval hospital

i saw a young marine, lanky,
tall, blond-haired texan paralyzed
from the neck down; regurgitating
digested rotted food due to shrapnel

i saw a young soldier wheeled
around the px with half a face
    missing

i saw young men blinded,
heads wrapped in gauze
being led by the arm
as they walk the halls

i saw the results of war after the fact,
convincing me the television shows
of my youth are false; where there
is no blood or dismemberment

i see a bone spur deferment
commander in chief
wanting a dictator-type parade
with tanks on our capital's streets;
playing tough,
never acknowledging
the personal devastation
he can unleash on our youth

or even caring

roots

a tree needs roots to thrive,
to grow, absorbing nutrients,
feeding the rings to widen
its girth, stretch its arms,
then drop its clothes in the
fall, covering the ground to
make mulch and replenish
the soil with nutrients, for
its seeds to start growing;
eventually replenishing
with new young saplings

in our lives, the family is the
root for many to grow
and prosper, feeding and
helping as best we can,
in the end, we are all trees

the right one

going for a walk
in the evening after dinner
i stroll down the street
enjoying the mild breeze
as the sun begins to set
painting homes in a warm
golden glow

crickets start to chirp
as I pass my neighbors
home, noticing
shutters closed
as the security van
drives past me
in the gated community

after fifty-two years With her
i am at peace with life, things
worked out nicely; the start
was rough with our parents
because we decided as teens
to have a runaway marriage
ignoring their protestations

sometimes you get lucky
in meeting the right one,
can't say it any more plainly

flames

their parents died in old age

after the funeral things settled down-
everyday life begins again;
on the weekend the four kids gathered
to clean out the parent's belongings

pictures, thousands of them,
boxes upon boxes overflowing-
the kids as newborns, starting school,
graduations, then their marriages,
            with some ex-spouses

the books of pictures under the bed
contain their parent's lives, whittled down
to a few collections. there are pictures of
their parents, grandparents plus old, faded,
crinkled ones of folks with no names,
            unfamiliar to anyone

they are gathered together.
each kid takes a few then
maybe one or two collections

leaving a large heap of memories
of multi-generations on the floor-
they go home, knowing the next day
the cleanout company is coming

memories fade in time,
forgotten-
many thrown in the trash,
eventually to go up in flames

lives lived,
lost to infinity;
just everyday people
just everyday people

the musician

her lyrical
single notes
play
on the strings
of his heart;
they merge
making music
which stirs
his passions

her love
reaches up,
deep into his soul

arms clinging
to her body,
wanting to be
forever
by her side,
playing
those singular notes
with him
again
forever

temptation

you look great
with what men want
when their hormones rage

hard to resist
the desire
when you smile
at me like that,
pursing your lips,
then licking them
with your tongue,
slowly

you go with anyone
who wants company,
on a whim,
then move on
to your next lover
without looking back
or caring

it is not love you want,
even permanence,
this i see as fact;
i do not want a side chick

in memoriam

please do not weep for me-
i had a good life,
found love, success, enjoyed
myself as i went along.
luck had a lot to do with it,
some say you make your own luck,
i do not know

i laughed a lot,
saw humor where others did not;
developed a crying heart
when sadness and problems
overcame strangers in life

in the end, i know some of you
will shed a tear or two for me,
some will laugh at the things
i said or did in life;
both are acceptable

my final words are
love someone, laugh a lot,
don't forget to be kind, and
charitable; then eat something
i'd enjoy, and share it with others

oh, one more thing-
be a mensch!
my father always
said it me to me;
it helps

why

why do people fall in love,
or pretend they are?
setting up hopes
for a relationship
then in secret
date others
hearts are broken,
lives destroyed,
never honest, or
true to love

left with children
after the divorce
her world turns
upside down,
her affirmation
of love discarded
as a used tissue

she is distraught

not enough money,
bills mounting up,
while he is off
mounting others;
she is a
loving mother
continuing her
commitment
to family;
working long hours
to support them

the ring

a wedding ring is a solid,
round symbol of a union
meant to last forever; made
of silver, gold or platinum

it is as indestructible
as a marriage should be,
the only thing, which can
remove it, is temptation

festering

i will love you forever-
his vows rang in her ears
many years before, now
only a memory at night

he is sleeping in another
woman's bed, somewhere,
his arms around her, kissing,
cuddling, whispering words of love

i will love you forever festers
in her gut, yelling out, alone at night,
screams of anguish, hatred, words
of murder, though only words, not action

reaching for the empty shot glass
she fills it again, hoping in the morning
her day will be brighter, new love will
appear, all will be normal again

female equality

smaller, petite, frail,
not as smart either;
words used to hold them
down since time began

unequal in many
religions, not allowed,
although i don't think
god differentiates

when prayers from the
devout are said, words are
the same, no difference
which gender says them

hypocrisy runs rampant
when illogic rules society,
time to hear them roar,
equal means equal period!

heartbreak

for six months
she carried her son
until birth, then years
of love, hugs, kisses

morning wake ups
with soft kisses
before breakfast,
then off to school

afternoon's homework,
sundays at church,
visits to grandmas,
christmas in pictures

i don't watch local news
anymore, too much death
and missing children
who were once loved

saying prayers for those
on tonight's tragic news,
deep in my heart, i know
it doesn't help, it's too late

scribbles

at the metropolitan museum of art
walking through the modern art floor
i am transfixed, mesmerized and motionless
standing in front of a few larger paintings

their lines, designs, and colors
grab me in a trance i cannot
look away from

how did they create such beauty
from abstract spaghetti lines
worth untold fortunes, to
hang on a wall amongst others

this bothered me

on my way home, i realized
my young grandchildren
do similar drawings in crayon;
if only they could sign them

same as us

wheelchair-bound
most of her life
some look at her
as damaged goods

lack of mobility
on two legs did
not affect her mind,
or break her spirit

she is capable
of having emotions,
experiencing love,
embracing it

her mind still works
as does her heart,
still capable of breaking
when he walks away

just like us

wheelchair-bound
most of her life
some look at her
as damaged goods

lack of mobility
on two legs did
not affect her brain,
or break her spirit

she is capable
of having emotions,
experiencing love,
embracing it

her mind still works
as does her heart,
it's capable of breaking
when he walks away

love happens

when roses bloom
your lips smile,
open eyes
reflect
the sun's warmth
in your heart,
the sweet honey
bees make from
kissing flowers
as tasty as your soul;
your gentle touch
reminds me of the
petal's velvet softness

love happens
when roses bloom

www.ingramcontent.com/pod-product-compliance
Lightning Source LLC
Chambersburg PA
CBHW061652180626
46818CB00003B/1059